HOPSCOTCH
ADVENTURES

Robin and the Friar

Tales of Robin Hood

First published in 2006 by
Franklin Watts
338 Euston Road
London
NW1 3BH

Franklin Watts Australia
Hachette Children's Books
Level 17/207 Kent Street
Sydney
NSW 2000

A CIP catalogue record for this book is available
from the British Library.

ISBN (10) 0 7496 6688 9 (hbk)
ISBN (13) 978-0-7496-6688-0 (hbk)
ISBN (10) 0 7496 6702 8 (pbk)
ISBN (13) 978-0-7496-6702-3 (pbk)

Series Editor: Jackie Hamley
Series Advisor: Dr Barrie Wade
Series Designer: Peter Scoulding

Printed in China

Franklin Watts is a division of
Hachette Children's Books.

Robin and
the Friar

by Damian Harvey and Martin Remphry

FRANKLIN WATTS
LONDON•SYDNEY

Sherwood Forest was filled with the clang of swords and the thud of arrows hitting their targets.

Robin Hood and his merry men were enjoying the summer's day.

Will Scarlet, Much the Miller's son and Little John were practising with their bows.

"I'm proud to have the best archers in the land," said Robin Hood.

But Will Scarlet laughed. "I hear there's a friar at Fountains Abbey who could beat us all!" he said.

"Then I'll not rest until I meet this friar!" cried Robin Hood.

9

Robin put on his chain-mail shirt,
picked up his sword and bow, then
set off for Fountains Abbey.

As Robin walked, he came across a
friar eating his lunch by the river.

"If you were a good man," said Robin Hood, "you'd carry me across this river."

The friar saw Robin's sword
and bow, and agreed to carry
him across.

When they reached the other side,
Robin Hood jumped to the ground.
Then the friar drew his sword.

"Now," said the friar, "you carry
me back so I can finish my lunch."
The friar's sword looked sharp,
so Robin agreed.

The water was cold and Robin

slipped and slithered on the stones.

At last they reached the other side
and the friar jumped to the ground.
The friar was about finish his lunch
when Robin drew his sword.

"Now," said Robin, "carry me
back or you will feel the point
of my sword."

Robin climbed onto the friar's shoulders and off they went.

But this time, the friar threw Robin into the water! "I hope you can swim," laughed the friar.

Robin Hood kicked and splashed
to the side of the river.

Then he drew his bow. "I'm going to pin your robes to that tree!" shouted Robin.

He took aim and fired an arrow, but the friar turned it away with his shield.

"Is that the best you can do?"

laughed the friar.

Robin fired another arrow.
But again the friar turned it
away. Robin fired until all
his arrows had gone.

"Now, draw your sword, friar!"
yelled Robin. Robin and the friar
fought all day, but neither one
could beat the other.

"That's enough!" cried Robin Hood. "You must be the friar of Fountains Abbey. I came looking for you!

"If you join me and my merry men in Sherwood Forest you'll have all the food you can eat and a new robe."

The friar looked at his tattered robe and nodded. "No man has stood against me before," he said. "I'll happily join you."

From that point on, Robin Hood and Friar Tuck became the best of friends.

31

Hopscotch has been specially designed to fit the requirements of the National Literacy Strategy. It offers real books by top authors and illustrators for children developing their reading skills. There are 37 Hopscotch stories to choose from:

Marvin, the Blue Pig
ISBN 0 7496 4619 5

Plip and Plop
ISBN 0 7496 4620 9

The Queen's Dragon
ISBN 0 7496 4618 7

Flora McQuack
ISBN 0 7496 4621 7

Willie the Whale
ISBN 0 7496 4623 3

Naughty Nancy
ISBN 0 7496 4622 5

Run!
ISBN 0 7496 4705 1

The Playground Snake
ISBN 0 7496 4706 X

"Sausages!"
ISBN 0 7496 4707 8

The Truth about Hansel and Gretel
ISBN 0 7496 4708 6

Pippin's Big Jump
ISBN 0 7496 4710 8

Whose Birthday Is It?
ISBN 0 7496 4709 4

The Princess and the Frog
ISBN 0 7496 5129 6

Flynn Flies High
ISBN 0 7496 5130 X

Clever Cat
ISBN 0 7496 5131 8

Moo!
ISBN 0 7496 5332 9

Izzie's Idea
ISBN 0 7496 5334 5

Roly-poly Rice Ball
ISBN 0 7496 5333 7

I Can't Stand It!
ISBN 0 7496 5765 0

Cockerel's Big Egg
ISBN 0 7496 5767 7

How to Teach a Dragon Manners
ISBN 0 7496 5873 8

The Truth about those Billy Goats
ISBN 0 7496 5766 9

Marlowe's Mum and the Tree House
ISBN 0 7496 5874 6

Bear in Town
ISBN 0 7496 5875 4

The Best Den Ever
ISBN 0 7496 5876 2

ADVENTURE STORIES

Aladdin and the Lamp
ISBN 0 7496 6678 1 *
ISBN 0 7496 6692 7

Blackbeard the Pirate
ISBN 0 7496 6676 5 *
ISBN 0 7496 6690 0

George and the Dragon
ISBN 0 7496 6677 3 *
ISBN 0 7496 6691 9

Jack the Giant-Killer
ISBN 0 7496 6680 3 *
ISBN 0 7496 6693 5

TALES OF KING ARTHUR

1. The Sword in the Stone
ISBN 0 7496 6681 1 *
ISBN 0 7496 6694 3

2. Arthur the King
ISBN 0 7496 6683 8 *
ISBN 0 7496 6695 1

3. The Round Table
ISBN 0 7496 6684 6 *
ISBN 0 7496 6697 8

4. Sir Lancelot and the Ice Castle
ISBN 0 7496 6685 4 *
ISBN 0 7496 6698 6

TALES OF ROBIN HOOD

Robin and the Knight
ISBN 0 7496 6686 2 *
ISBN 0 7496 6699 4

Robin and the Monk
ISBN 0 7496 6687 0 *
ISBN 0 7496 6700 1

Robin and the Friar
ISBN 0 7496 6688 9 *
ISBN 0 7496 6702 8

Robin and the Silver Arrow
ISBN 0 7496 6689 7 *
ISBN 0 7496 6703 6

* **hardback**